THIS WALKER BOOK BELONGS TO:

_____

_____

_____

For Megan

First published 2003 by Walker Books Ltd
87 Vauxhall Walk, London SE11 5HJ

This edition including DVD published 2007

4 6 8 10 9 7 5

Printed in China

British Library Cataloguing in Publication Data: a catalogue record
for this book is available from the British Library

ISBN 978-1-4063-0743-6

www.walkerbooks.co.uk

The Ravenous Beast

Niamh Sharkey

WALKER BOOKS
AND SUBSIDIARIES
LONDON • BOSTON • SYDNEY • AUCKLAND

"I AM

THE HUNGRIEST

ANIMAL OF ALL,"

said the Ravenous Beast.
"I'm hungry, hungry, hungry!
I'm so hungry I could eat

the big yellow house on the hill.

Gobble it up! Swallow it down!

Now THAT'S what I call hungry!"

"Nonsense! Smonsense!"
said the little white mouse.
"No one's hungrier than me.
I'm so hungry I could eat

a red boat and a ringing bell.

Nibble nibble! Tuck 'em away!

Now THAT'S what
I call hungry!"

"Hokum! Pokum!"

said the marmalade cat. "I'm as hungry as can be. I'm so hungry I could eat

a bucket, a spade and some red lemonade.

Gnaw 'em! Gulp 'em! Stuff 'em down!

Now THAT'S what I call hungry!"

"Hooey!
Phooey!"
said the spotty dog.
"No one's hungrier than me.
I'm so hungry I could eat

a roller skate, a birthday cake,
a rubber duck, a ticking clock.

Slurp 'em! Burp 'em! Woof 'em down!
Now THAT'S what
I call hungry!"

"Moo! Moo! Malarkey!" said the black-and-white cow. "I'm as hungry as can be. I'm so hungry I could eat

a castle, a crown, the Queen's dressing-gown, a wellie-boot, all the King's loot.

Munch 'em up! Crunch 'em down!

Now THAT'S what I call hungry!"

"Balderdash!
Baloney!"

said the green crocodile.
"No one's hungrier than me.
I'm so hungry I could eat

a suitcase, a wand, a Jack-in-the-box,

a polka-dot sock, a top hat and a spinning top.

Snip 'em up! Snap 'em down!

Now THAT'S what I call

hungry!"

"Flip! Flap-doodle!"
said the grinning lion.
"I'm as hungry as can be.
I'm so hungry I could eat

a ray gun, a rocket,
a humbug from my pocket,
a trampoline, a trombone with a dent,
a bouncing ball, a circus tent.

Bite 'em up! Bolt 'em down!
Now THAT'S
what I call
hungry!"

"**Not on your nelly!**"
said the big-eared elephant.
"No one's hungrier than me.
I'm so hungry I could eat

an aeroplane, a parachute,
a pot of tea, a hot-air balloon,
a tin of beans, a parcel, a kite and a green bus.

Suck 'em up! Scoff 'em down!

Now THAT'S what
I call hungry!"

"Whoosh! Swoosh!"

said the gigantic whale.
"I'm as hungry as can be.
I'm so hungry I could eat

a pirate's ship, a treasure map,
a piggy bank, a yellow mac, an anchor, a chain,
a flag, a tin drum, yo-ho-ho and a barrel of rum.

Squish 'em in! Squash 'em down!

Now THAT'S what I

call hungry!"

"STOP!"
said the Ravenous Beast.

"I AM the HUNGRIEST of all!

I'm so hungry I'm going to eat

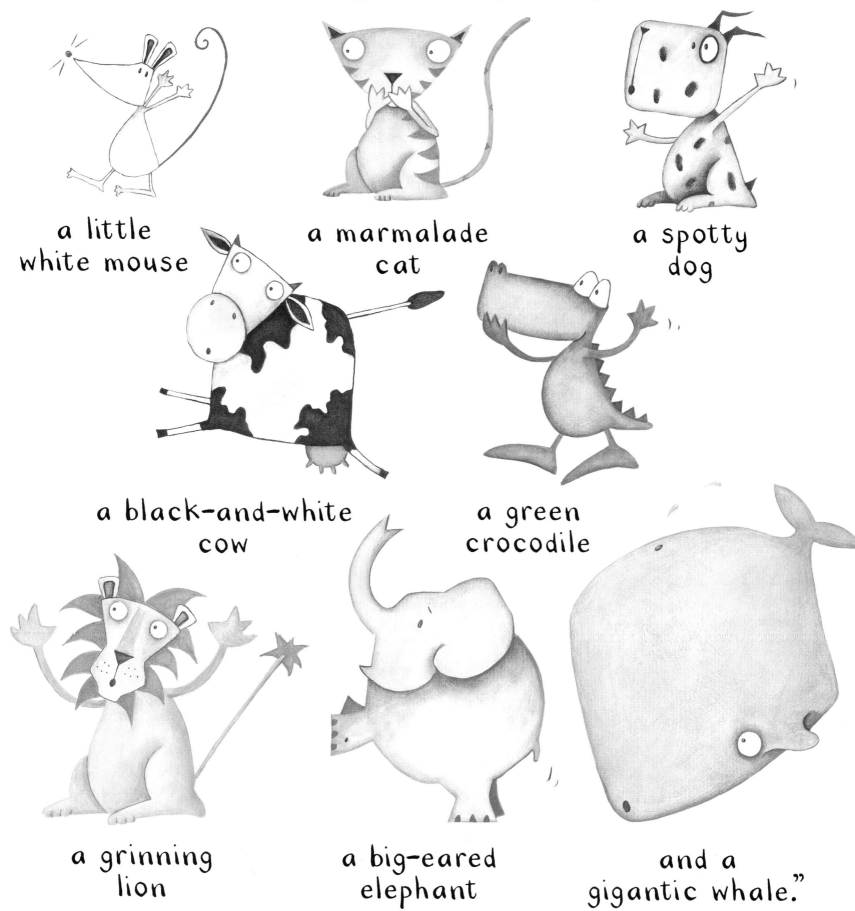

a little
white mouse

a marmalade
cat

a spotty
dog

a black-and-white
cow

a green
crocodile

a grinning
lion

a big-eared
elephant

and a
gigantic whale."

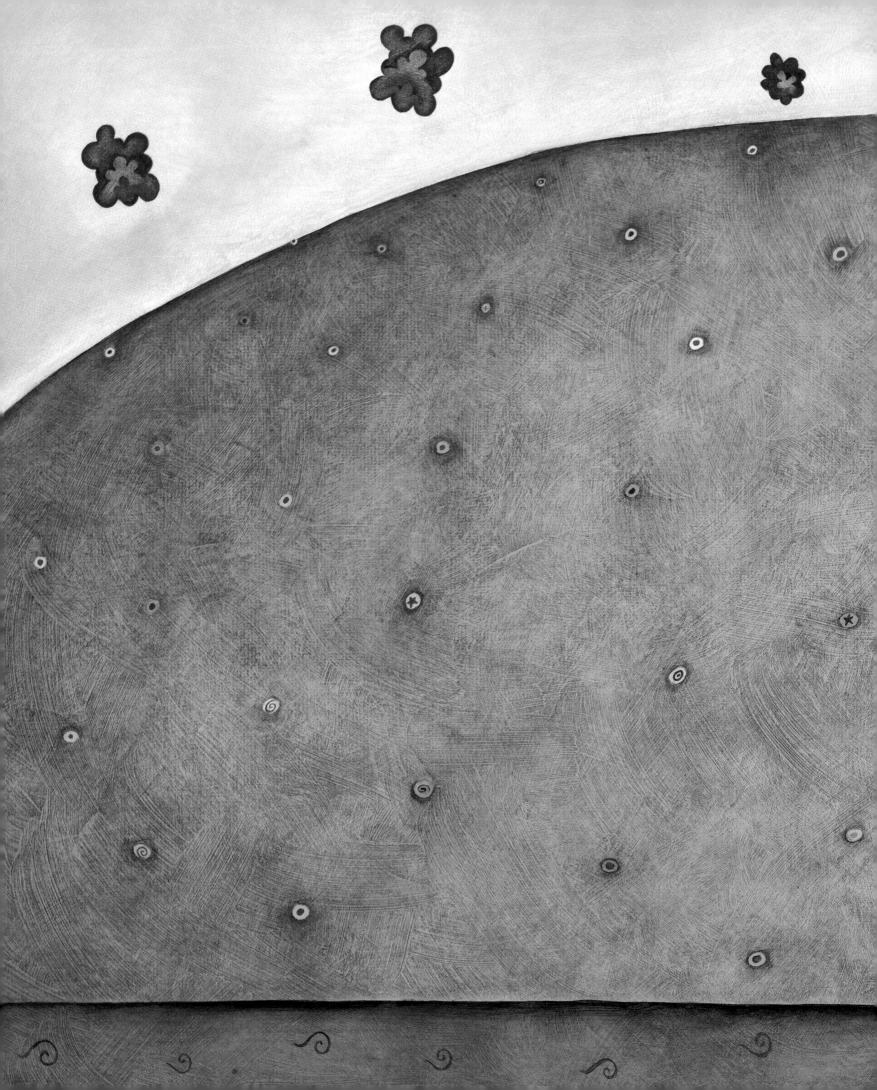

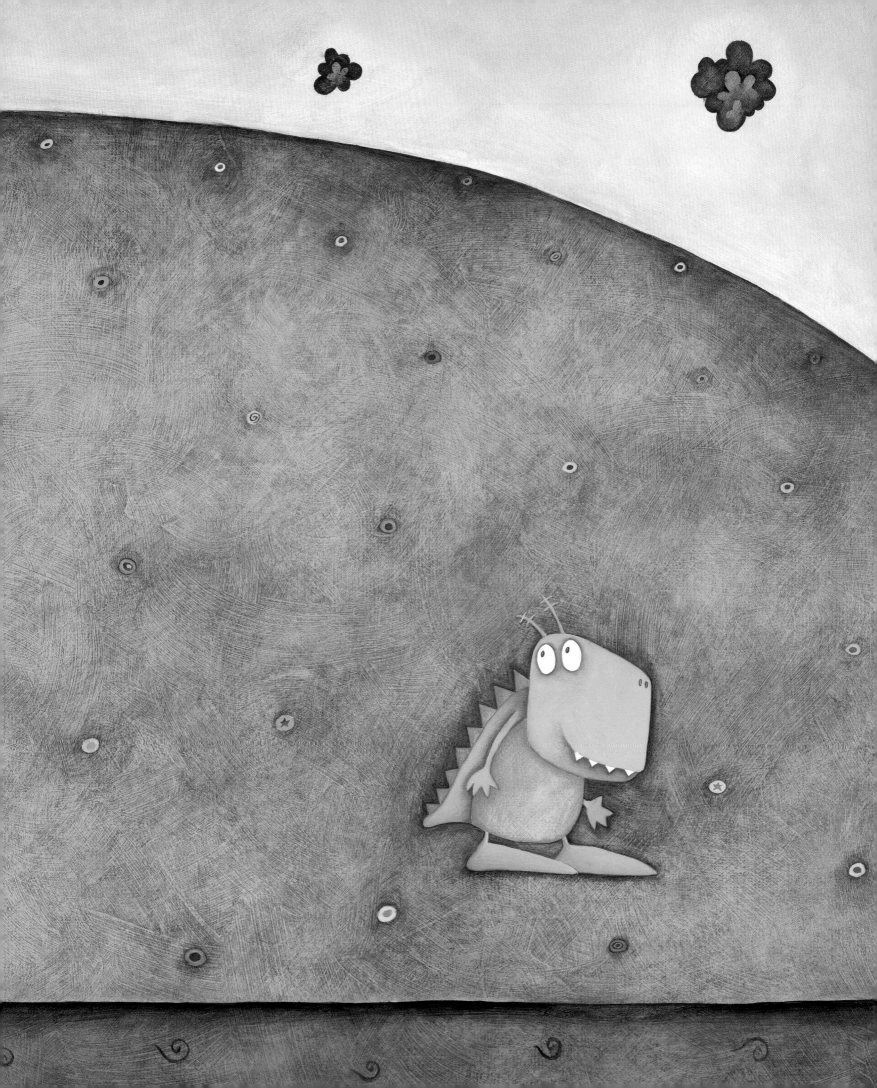